Sea Crow

For Gabrielle and Jacob,
my beachcombers
S.S.

For Jim Simpson
L.M

Sea Crow

Story by Shannon Stewart

Illustrations by Liz Milkau

ORCA BOOK PUBLISHERS

One day Jessica moved into a new house close to the sea.

On the first night she slept in one of the bare upstairs rooms with her little brother, Miles. Jessica and Miles lay awake for a long time.

"What are you afraid of?" Jessica asked her brother.

"Boxes," said Miles. "And witches."

"Me too," said Jessica. But she didn't say what she was really afraid of.

Miles was lucky. He was too little for school.

Out the window Jessica saw the shadows of enormous black trees arching in the wind. She strained to hear the ocean at the end of their street.

"And pickles," said Miles.

"Pickles?" asked Jessica.

"Yes. Pickles are scary." Miles shivered and fell asleep.

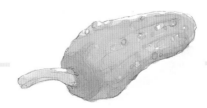

The next morning was sunny and cool. Jessica couldn't find her favorite pair of overalls or the hairbrush that didn't snag her tangles. Her father said she had to go to school anyway.

Her new teacher, Ms. Ping, smiled and shook her hand. She showed Jessica where she could sit at her own desk, between Alicia and Mark.

"We're happy to have you in our classroom," said Ms. Ping.

Jessica nodded and sat down.

"We have Show and Tell for fifteen minutes every morning," said Ms. Ping. "Today you can listen, and when you feel like it, you can share something with us, okay?"

Jessica nodded again.

A boy named Toby showed a picture he had made using leaves and small pebbles. A girl named Patricia spoke about her favorite book, which had giant pictures of horses inside. By the time a girl named Sarah showed a big, blue bruise on her leg that she had gotten from falling off her bike, Jessica had begun to cry.

At lunch, Jessica's mother and Miles came to walk her home.

"Are you scared?" asked Miles when he saw her.

Jessica said nothing.

"I saw a monster in a box," said Miles. "And a dragon. But I didn't see any pickles."

"First days at new schools are always hard," said her mother, putting her arm around Jessica.

At home they packed cheese, crackers, apples and marshmallows for a picnic lunch at the beach.

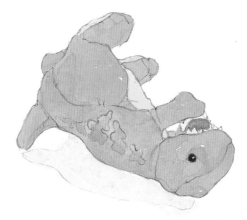

Jessica had never seen the beach at low tide. Large stones near the edge of the water were covered in slippery seaweed. When Jessica rolled the heavy stones away, a flurry of tiny crabs, some no bigger than her smallest fingernail, scurried off to hide. Miles squealed when he saw them.

"Scary spiders!" he cried. "I don't like them!"

"Not spiders, Miles. They're crabs. Do you want to hold one?" Jessica plucked some of the smaller crabs from between the stones and held them out to Miles on the palm of her hand.

Jessica loved the beach.

She saw a seagull pry a purple starfish from the shallows and fly away with it in its beak. She loved the salty fish smell of the air and the giant bulbs of kelp seaweed that she could pop with a bang under her foot.

"You're going to be late for school!" called Jessica's mother. Jessica dragged two long strands of kelp up the street and left them in her garden.

"What are they for?" asked Miles.

"I like them," said Jessica. "That's all."

All week long, Jessica thought of the beach.

Ms. Ping wrote math sums on the board, and Jessica thought of thousands of barnacles opening their mouths when the tide came in. She played at Alicia's house and drew pictures of bright starfish and deep blue oceans filled with fish. When it was Show and Tell, Jessica thought of lifting the biggest stone on the beach and finding shiny crabs underneath, snapping their pincers at the air.

"Jessica, would you like to share anything for Show and Tell tomorrow?" Ms. Ping asked.

"No, that's okay," said Jessica.

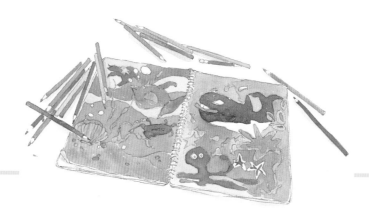

Jessica's room was set up now. Her favorite overalls were hanging in her cupboard. But it still didn't feel like home.

Sometimes Miles visited at night.

"I'm scared," he said.

"What are you scared of?" asked Jessica.

"Goblins," said Miles. "And spiders and my tennis ball."

"Why are you afraid of your tennis ball?" asked Jessica.

"Because it's furry," said Miles. Jessica told Miles he could sleep beside her if he promised not to hog her blanket.

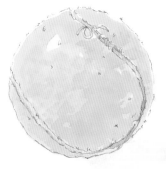

Whenever they went down to the beach, Jessica and Miles brought something home: smooth driftwood; piles of clam shells, oyster shells, mussel shells and old, broken crab shells; stones and pieces of green and brown glass worn smooth by the sand and the water; all sorts of seaweed that had dried into hard black snakes in the sun; pieces of rope and long feathers from seagulls and crows.

"What are you going to do with all this stuff?" asked Jessica's parents.

Jessica wasn't sure.

She liked the beach more than anything. One evening, a large crab pinched her finger in its thick front claw. Jessica dropped it in surprise.

"Crabs are scary," said Miles, watching her.

"No they're not. They're just protecting themselves. See, Miles, their skeleton is on the outside of their body. Our skeletons are inside us."

"Skeletons are scary," said Miles. "Ghosts too."

Jessica looked at Miles and he looked at her.

"You're not scary, Jessica."

"Of course not," said Jessica, and she brought home some old flat boards that had been pounded by the waves.

The next day was hot. Jessica wore her overalls to school and thought about the pile of beach treasure waiting in her garden. After school she invited Alicia home.

Jessica and Alicia and Miles tied and hammered driftwood and boards together until they had a shape that looked like a body with arms and legs and a head. They glued shells, glass and pebbles onto long strands of seaweed and draped these around the arms and body to make a black, serpentine robe. Leftover seaweed became a tangle of hair, and two white clamshell eyes sparkled on the face. Miles chose a mussel shell for a nose, and Alicia used empty, curved crab legs to make a mouth. A ring of seagull feathers crowned the head.

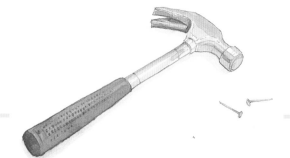

"Who is she?" asked Miles, open-mouthed, when they had finished.

"Sea Crow," said Jessica.

"She's scary-looking!" said Miles.

"She's not a scarecrow, Miles. She's Sea Crow. If you tell her what frightens you, she will make you feel better."

Miles stared at the creature covered in shells and seaweed.

"Try it," said Jessica. "What makes you scared?"

"Pickles?" squeaked Miles.

"And…?"

"Goblins and ghosts and pirates and monsters and barbers and hospitals and crusts and toilet noises and stripes," said Miles.

"Stripes?" asked Alicia.

"Zebra stripes," said Miles, gulping.

"Your turn, Alicia," said Jessica.

"Ummm…," said Alicia. "Wild bears, I guess. Thunderstorms. Sometimes the dark."

Alicia looked at Jessica. "What about you?"

"New homes," said Jessica. "New schools and new people."

Sea Crow's seaweed cape and feather crown quivered. Beach glass and clam shells rattled in the wind.

"Sea Crow's saying something," said Miles. "Wow!"

The next morning was hot and sunny. Jessica decided to wear shorts instead of overalls.

"Do you want me to walk you to school?" her father asked.

"That's okay. Alicia is coming by. We're going together."

"Are you sure?" said her mother.

"Sure," said Jessica.

"See you! Goodbye!" said Miles at the door.

Alicia stared as Jessica walked down the steps. "What happened to your leg?" she asked.

"When I was born I was missing my right leg," said Jessica, "so the doctors made me an artificial one."

"Wow!" said Alicia. "What does it feel like? Does it hurt?"

"No," Jessica said. "It feels just fine."

As the girls walked down the road to school, Sea Crow stirred in the morning sun.

National Library of Canada Cataloguing in Publication Data

Stewart, Shannon, 1966-

Sea Crow / story by Shannon Stewart; illustrations by Liz Milkau.

ISBN 1-55143-288-9
1. Children with disabilities--Juvenile fiction. I. Milkau, Liz II. Title.

PS8587.T4894S52 2004   jC813'.54   C2003-907399-8

Library of Congress Control Number: 2003116364

Summary: Jessica's love of the beach, just down the road from her
new home, helps her and her younger brother to overcome their fears.

Orca Book Publishers gratefully acknowledges the support of its publishing
program provided by the following agencies: the Department of Canadian
Heritage, the Canada Council for the Arts, and the British Columbia Arts Council.

Design by Christine Toller/Lynn O'Rourke
Printed and bound in Hong Kong

Orca Book Publishers
1030 North Park Street
Victoria, BC Canada
V8T 1C6

Orca Book Publishers
PO Box 468
Custer, WA USA
98240-0468

06 05 04 04 • 5 4 3 2 1